AF506807

Tales From Behind Your Wall of Dreams

by

David Bongianino

DORRANCE
PUBLISHING CO
EST. 1920
PITTSBURGH, PENNSYLVANIA 15238

The contents of this work, including, but not limited to, the accuracy of events, people, and places depicted; opinions expressed; permission to use previously published materials included; and any advice given or actions advocated are solely the responsibility of the author, who assumes all liability for said work and indemnifies the publisher against any claims stemming from publication of the work.

All Rights Reserved
Copyright © 2023 by Dave Bongianino

No part of this book may be reproduced or transmitted, downloaded, distributed, reverse engineered, or stored in or introduced into any information storage and retrieval system, in any form or by any means, including photocopying and recording, whether electronic or mechanical, now known or hereinafter invented without permission in writing from the publisher.

Dorrance Publishing Co
585 Alpha Drive
Pittsburgh, PA 15238
Visit our website at www.dorrancebookstore.com

ISBN: 979-8-88729-343-1
eISBN: 979-8-88729-843-6

DEDICATION

Is it ever too late to say I'm sorry
or to whisper, I love you, softly
If I could go back and change
just one of my many mistakes
time hasn't been kind and in my mind
their faces begin to fade
I've kept the memory alive
even though it's been a long time
the thought of them brings a tear to my eye
I know I was wrong
because life isn't always long
whether their ashes are spread in some obscure place
or I kneel and put roses on their grave
one is the reason I'm alive
one is the reason I write
what I didn't do or what I didn't say
my mistakes
even though there were many priceless moments
I consider them all golden
It's blame and shame I'm left holding
whether it's hours, minutes, or seconds
when I wasn't there, that's what I'm regretting
you were in poor health
but I was too busy feeling sorry for myself
and now it's me who needs forgiving
because death is truly hardest on the living
how can I say what I did not say or do

what I did not do how many times I wished to trade places
    with you
then maybe, I could let go of my mistakes
but instead, I write these pages
and honor you in memory and name
you will live forever even after I fade
because you deserve much more than I gave

In loving memory of
Marlene J. Bongianino
Dante M. Bongianino

It's never too late to say I'm sorry
or whisper, I love you, softly

Introduction

Centuries ago, the Gods chose a monster to secure the gates
    of hell
one can only imagine the stories he could tell
Alas he cannot speak
imagination, the unspoken word, if it's the truth you seek
you can not combat evil with virtue
kindness is a weakness that will haunt you
the meek will inherit the earth is only a myth
the meek with have what is left
when the strong are done with it
right, wrong does not apply
carry morals into battle and you will die
the beast is the son of every man
in the garden of Eden he held the serpent in his hand
he was justice before time began
his eyes tell the story of a tortured soul
they can cut like knives or make diamonds from coal
the beast of legend and lure
keeping our gates secure
when our monsters and demons invade our dreams
they come alive and have the urge to feed
these monsters our dreams create
are looking for portals in which to escape
our nightmares are prisms that demons create
you shiver, you shake, you inevitably awake
but now it's too late
what you have conjured in your sleep
is now alive and bearing its teeth

pray for your soul to keep
call upon the beast to return these demons to your dreams
you can now awake, feeling safe
the beast with the flaming knives
has kept your demons inside
for one more night
good versus evil is only a fairy tale
the Gods chose a monster to guard the gates of hell
one can only imagine the stories he could tell

Blood Wolf Moon

The story is as old as the land
On which it began
The moon possesses great power
Foreign to the men who inhabit the earth
Whether it be legend, myth, or curse
Tales told around fires by those who were here first
When our demons and monsters invade our dreams
They come alive and have the urge to feed
Listen to the trees, and you will hear
The sound of men becoming what they fear
Prophecy consumed by the years
We search endlessly for the truth
The end could be coming, all too soon
Heed the warning of the blood wolf moon

A native Alaskan, Calian (Indian for warrior) or Cal as his friends call him, was the son of a pipeline worker from Utah. His father never married his mother, a native Alaskan herself from the Village of Point Barrow (Utqiagvik), the northernmost city in Alaska. This is where Cal was raised after his father moved back the lower 48 and where the story begins. Cal's father stayed in touch and sent regular checks for his support. Cal showed early in his life that he was intelligent and athletic. The star of his high school football team and honor student as well. His mother wanted a better life for him than Point Barrow could offer, so she arranged for him to move to Utah and live with his birth father. College recruiters began to hear of his abilities, and by his senior year, he had received many scholarship offers, in the end choosing to stay at home and the University of Utah. Excelling at sports all his life, Cal briefly entertained the idea of becoming a professional athlete, but his small-town upbringing made for an internal conflict that was consuming. He loved the land and had a fondness for all living creatures, and because of his athletic ability, he was given the opportunity to study agriculture, thus the conflict. While attending a pep rally, he was introduced to the girl who would become his future wife. Kris, a biology major, took one look at Cal and knew he would be her future husband. She spent many hours listening to his stories of the quaint little town of Point Barrow, Alaska and fell in love with the idea of moving there and working a patch of land. His father tried to convince him to try the NFL or maybe Canadian football, but Cal's mind was made, and upon graduation, he and Kris said their goodbyes.

Kris was enchanted by the folklore and atmosphere surrounding the community of Point Barrow, or Utqiagvik, as it was formerly known. The natives were friendly and inviting, hard-working people who made her feel right at home. She felt safe, happy. Point Barrow was not a place to homestead; it was a place with history and stories, Cal's past. However, what they wanted was to build a home from the ground up and experience life like his ancestors. Cal's mother knew her son, knew he would not be satisfied with a rural home and a nine-to-five job. She suggested Kodiak Island, about 1,000 miles south of Point Barrow. Kodiak Island is the ancestral land of the Sugpiaq. About 13,000 people live on the island. There would be homestead land available, but that was a hard life for anyone. It was early February, temperatures could drop to -25 degrees at night, but Cal chartered a plane for him and Kris to begin their journey of self-discovery. Kodiak was mostly a fishing hole, but hunting was good as well, especially in the northern part of the island. Preferring fishing to hunting bear, they chose the southern part. Even though he was on a full ride at Utah, Cal still worked and saved almost every dime he made in the four years at college; it was how he was raised. Kris had a small savings as well, so together they were able to purchase a 20-acre parcel of undeveloped land. They flew back to Point Barrow to get the rest of their belongings and say goodbye to his mom.

Flying was the only way to get to the island, so they traveled light, purchasing supplies on Kodiak. The barest of necessities would include tools for building, food, a radio, a temporary living structure (tent), and one more thing. Cal had his eye on a snowmobile, but it was not in his budget. The store owner offered credit or trade for fresh fish or Caribou meat. Thinking and tempted but he declined the offer, choosing a Winchester rifle instead, telling the owner he would be back soon to get the snowmobile. Kris had her eye on a one-year-old Husky dog that needed a good home. Miska, Eskimo for little bear, was the dog's name. Kris looked at Cal and he just smiled. The three of them made their way to their new home. It was early April on Kodiak Island, days were longer, work was endless. They could see up to six inches of fresh snow and the temperature could plummet to -14 at night. Acclimating to the conditions is hard on one's body and mind, but these were two young, strong kids, determined. The tent provided some shelter, living much like the Indians did at one time, and they began to build around it with the abundance of timber on the property. The working hut had a working fireplace and a stove; some would say it was both at once. A bed and a backroom nature's call, not bad for the short time they had been here. Wherever Kris laid, Miska did as well; sometimes Cal had to fight for an inch of space on the bed. Exhausted most nights, they could all sleep just about anywhere. Sleep, per chance to, Kris was startled and awakened by the sound of her beloved Miska barking. Cal was dead asleep, did not budge. Kris felt for her dog, but he was not there; she sensed something was not right. Opening the door to the hut, she ran towards the sound of the dog barking. The moon was bright enough to illuminate the entire area and Kris quickly found her Miska face-to-face with a wolf. A large, black wolf. Panicked and shaken, she began yelling and waving her arms, hoping this would scare off the wolf. The yelling woke Cal; grabbing his rifle, he ran towards the noise. The moon was a bright red, as red as the blood on the ground around Kris, who was holding a very still Miska. Not knowing whose blood it was or how badly the dog was hurt, Cal just helped Kris to her feet, gave her the gun, and picked Miska up, carrying him to the hut. Kris didn't even realize she too had been bitten. It was the middle of the night and the chances of getting a chopper out there now was not good. Kris was more concerned for her dog than herself. Cal was concerned for both, applying makeshift bandages to Miska's wounds all the while Kris explained what transpired. The fear of rabies was all that ran through Cal's mind and the fact that neither of them ever considered a first-aid kit as a priority. Cal remembered some home remedies his mother used on him as a kid, but nothing ever about a wolf bite. These remedies could be found in the area, but he would have to wait for daylight and even then, no guarantees. Sleep now was out of the question for him, but Kris and Miska were already fast asleep. At first light, Cal radioed for a chopper. Miska woke and began licking Kris's face. They both seemed fine, considering the events that took place under that bright red moon. The helicopter found a place to land, and soon after, Cal and Kris were on their way to Providence Hospital in Kodiak.

The nurse at Providence Hospital asked what had happened while looking at the bite on Kris's arm. Cal just observed. The bite was not infected and no early signs of rabies, but tests would still have to be run. When the doctor came in, he was all business, not even acknowledging Cal. He asked if the nurse had taken a blood sample yet and if anyone else were bitten, still not even looking at Cal. Kris said that her dog has a couple of scratches, she looked over at Cal knowing that was a lie. The doctor then turned his attention to Cal, coldly suggesting the dog be put down. Kris became visibly agitated by the nerve and pulled her arm away from the doctor. The doctor ordered the first in a series of rabies shots even before the results of any tests were given. The doctor left abruptly while the nurse reentered the room with what she said was an Immune Globulin shot that she administered to Kris. For some reason, Kris trusted the nurse. There were to be four more shots given over a period of 14 days. Cal knew it would be difficult for them to return for the shots and asked if there were any way he could get the shots and administer them himself. Kris was anxious to get back and check on Miska, but Cal was concerned about the next four shots and how he was going to work that out. Kris got up and left the room, telling Cal she would be waiting outside for him. Cal had to find the doctor or the nurse for instructions on what to do next for Kris. Neither could be found. Now Cal was getting anxious, and a bit agitated himself. He found another nurse and began to tell his story to her; she interrupted and told him that the shots were easy to do, but he would have to go to the pharmacy with the prescription. The pharmacy was a short walk from the hospital, but Cal didn't want Kris to have to exert herself right now, so he suggested she wait while he retrieved the medicine. She was adamant that she return to Miska as soon as possible. The nurse overheard the conversation and told them the chopper pilot was her boyfriend and he would be happy to fly Kris back to the homestead. This was the best possible news for all and so it was settled. The short walk to the pharmacy turned out to be a hell of a lot longer than Cal was comfortable with, but the things we do for love. Kodiak was not a big place, but sometimes when you're in a hurry, a few minutes seems like hours. Many thoughts ran through his head as he approached what had to be the pharmacy, even though it looked more like a five and dime store. Cal had little money on him and wondered how this was going to work as he opened the front door. An old man smoking an even older pipe sat behind the counter, never got up or even spoke. Cal told him who he was and why he was there, and then began to explain how he was going to pay. The old man said his name was Vitus; it was Danish. He asked if Cal could sit for a minute. Confused and in a big hurry, Cal reluctantly agreed. Vitus asked who had been bitten. Cal replied, his wife, and then asked when the prescription would be ready and how much it would cost. Vitus ignored the question and began to tell a story. Kodiak wasn't always an island; it was settled in 1741 by the Russians. There were about 30 people that formed two tribes. Not like Indian tribes with a chief and tomahawks and such, but what else would you call them. They owned slaves that were coastal Indians from the southeast. A custom carried over from the war. Cal interrupted with an angry tone, wanting to know who ran this pharmacy. Vitus continued the story, telling of his great-grandfather who was Vitus Bering, a Dane as well. There was fishing, hunting, trapping, and trade. Trading slaves as well as furs and meat. His great-grandmother was a 13-year-old Indian slave sold to his great-grandfather for a blanket and a horse. There was a pact made as well, one honored by both tribes. Cal had enough and got up to walk out. Vitus continued anyway with his voice getting more deliberate. He said that his great-grandfather had two boys with the Indian slave. One was five, the other three when it happened. This got Cal's attention for some reason, perhaps desperation. Vitus said one night under the blood moon, a wolf attacked his wife and sons. Vitus said his great-grandfather would be gone for days hunting. On this night, he returned to an empty hut. Behind the hut, he saw footprints in the snow, and tracks, wolf tracks. It appeared as though the wolf was dragging something, and the footprints were following. About 200 yards from the hut, he came upon his wife and two boys covered in blood. He helped them back to the hut and got them cleaned up. The oldest boy was not harmed, but the youngest and his wife were badly bitten. Cal was not leaving now. Vitus said days later, the young son died from the wounds he sustained. His great-grandfather hunted the wolf for days, but it was if it disappeared. By this time, his great-grandmother had taken seriously ill; rabies was suspected. Fevered, confused, madness would surely be next, and then a painful death. There were no vaccines, and no home remedies were effective. Great-grandfather had to get help, so he got on his horse, leaving his five-year-old son with his ailing wife. The only other tribe was a day's ride, but he had no other option. These tribes turned into villages and communities in 1827, but for now, they were guarded and superstitious like the old ways. Great-grandpa knew these people because he traded with them regularly. When Great-grandpa arrived, he was welcomed, but that welcome would turn cold when he explained what had happened to his family. These tribes have elders, and they speak for everyone; they are law. The elder was of Russian descent and coldly pronounced death to my great-grandma and the boy. Putting them down like dogs. He warned my great-grandpa of the Omega wolf or lone wolf. The Omega operates outside the pack, until the pack returns, and then the Omega must submit to the Alpha or die. The Omega that bit my great-grandma will stay in the area and come back for her. She is his now; she will bring him food, offerings, sacrifices to prove her loyalty. She will submit to him, and they will leave together, never to be seen again. The pack will come for them both; they will both submit to the Alpha or die. Anyone or anything in the pack's way will die. It was Russian folklore, and it was law. My great-grandpa refused to kill his wife and son; he asked if there were any other way. The elder hesitated but responded by telling my great-grandpa to kill the Omega under the blood moon and his blood will be given to your wife and son. This act will break the curse and the cycle. The Omega dead, your wife clean, the pack will not come. Cal realized there was no medicine, just a message from a senile old man and so much time had been wasted. Vitus knew he was losing his audience, but continued hoping some of this would convince Cal. Upon arriving at his homestead, my great-grandpa felt something was wrong. He jumped off his horse and began walking with gun in hand. He hollered for his family, but no response. It was night and the moon was orangish red. The blood moon, there were four total lunar eclipses that happened in a span of two years. Six months apart with five uneclipsed, full moons in between. Some say it was the hunter's moon; some say it was the second coming of Jesus, the end of days. Cal knew this because he was a native of Point Barrow. He said it was the lunar Tetred. Vitus continued: his great-grandpa looked inside the hut, found no one. Walked around the back, no one. He found footprints in the fresh snow. It was April, six inches of fresh snow and the temperature was dropping into the teens. These footprints were human, barefoot in the freezing cold. How bad could things have gotten for his bride to be barefoot outside? He quickened his pace, calling out as he ran until he discovered in the distance, his naked wife covered in blood. No sign of his son. He called to her, but she was in a state of shock or madness; upon reaching her, her eyes were glazed over. Taking on almost a gold glow. Grandpa asked about the son, but she just laughed and said he will be pleased, he will be pleased. He's coming for me, he's coming for me, laughing all the while. Grandpa picked her up and took her back to the hut, wrapped her in a blanket, and started a fire. Out of patience with Great-grandma, Great-grandpa wanted answers, wanted to know the whereabouts of his son. He tied her hands to the bed despite her condition; he just didn't trust her anymore. He went to look for his son. He followed the tracks again, and this time he noticed where they stopped, knelt down, and moved away some fresh snow to find a hole; there he found his son, alive. While only minutes had passed, Cal felt this old man had taken enough of his time, and the moral of this story is that his great-grandma had rabies and went insane. At least that's what he was telling himself, so as to face the reality of this story hitting close to home. Cal wanted to leave but needed to hear more. Vitus said his great-grandpa took his son back to the hut only to find his wife had gotten free and now was attacking him, scratching, clawing, biting, and howling like a mad dog. He hit with a right cross that sent her to the floor; once down, he staked her to the ground, remembering what the elder said to him about the blood of the Omega wolf. Knowing the wolf was still close, he grabbed his rifle and his son, and went after the wolf. Tracking him in the fresh snow would be easy. Cal interrupted again, believing he knew the ending to this story. But he did not. Vitus said his great-grandpa never found the wolf; tired, hungry, and worried about his son, they turned back to the hut. The smell of smoke filled the air, and when the hut was in view, he could see it burning. The tribe had come while he was gone and burned the hut to the ground with my great grandmother in it. She was a pile of bones when my grandfather found her. That five-year-old boy was my grandfather and he told me that story when I was five. The settlers believed in the curse, and they were just protecting themselves. The moon possesses great power, foreign to the men that inhabit this earth. Cal argued that there are no wolves on Kodiak Island. Vitus argued, except the one that bit your wife. Cal said this is a story and the only difference between the truth and an urban legend is how many times it's repeated. Vitus told him that Kodiak was once part of the mainland, but Fenrin, the God of wolves, chased the wolves out of Kodiak, and her and Lupa, son of Loki, pushed Kodiak into the sea, so they could not come back. Cal laughed and headed for the door. Vitus asked if he believed that Moses parted the red sea, if he believed Sampson killed 100 soldiers with the jawbone of an ass. Do you believe Jesus Christ died on the cross and then came back to life? If you believe those stories because of faith, why not this story? Cal was gone now, but that didn't stop Vitus from preaching. There is a blood moon tonight, kill the Omega before he takes your wife... and son. Before the pack comes for us all. Listen for the cry of the pack, they're coming, they're coming.

Cal was nervous and anxious now because of the time spent with a crazy old man instead of his injured wife. It didn't seem to take nearly as much time to walk back to the hospital as it did to walk to the so-called pharmacy, He arrived at the hospital looking for the doctor but instead found the nurse that treated Kris. She was very apologetic about the whole ordeal, but she insisted that Cal follow her to quiet place to talk. Cal was furious and done talking. He demanded to see the doctor and wanted the shots for his wife. The nurse told him the shots were useless and that the doctor shouldn't have mislead him that way. But Cal needed to hear the story and he would not have agreed to go if he knew. The nurse continued to tell him that the first shot was a placebo, just to buy some time. She told him that she knows how all of this sounds, but there is one more thing, the results of the blood test. The test results indicated that the blood that she drew personally from his wife's arm was not human blood; it was canine. Cal asked if everyone in this town was crazy. The nurse told him go to his wife and follow the instructions that Vitus gave him. It may sound insane now, but there will come a time in the not too distant future where the insane will save your life. Cal said Vitus is a crazy old man and you people should be ashamed of yourselves. The nurse said you won't make it back to your homestead in time; she hands him the keys to her truck and wished him good luck. As he drove the fifty some miles back to his home, he couldn't help but notice the eerie similarities in the story and the attack on Kris. The nurse let him use her truck; she didn't even know him. It was all surreal. There was a fresh snow that day and on into the night, about eight inches in all. Cal stopped the truck along the road because plows didn't come out this far. He would walk another mile or so to the hut; the temperature was falling, and the moon was a bright orange. The blood moon. As he got closer to his home, he began to call out Kris, hoping she would respond or Miska would come running to him. No answer, he got to the door and no one, no Kris, no Miska. He called again, and again; out of nowhere she appeared, startling him. He was pleased to see her and immediately asked how she was feeling. She did not answer, she just came closer and the look in her eyes was one he knew all too well. She was craving affection. She still did not speak; she just started undressing him. Cal wanted to know if she were up for this, but she just kept taking off his clothes and then hers. Kris was normally shy when it came to sex, reserved, Cal made the first move when he saw that look. She was not shy or reserved now; she was aggressive and in complete control. She pushed him down onto the bed and began to mount him, again out of character for her. Cal did not object though; he was just glad to see her and know she was alright. As the sex progressed, she became more aggressive, even violent. He had to stop her on many occasions because she was hurting him. Even drawing blood on his lip from biting to hard, there were scratches on his back. He was worn out from the events of the day and Kris's overtly new sexual appetite. They both rolled over and went to sleep for what seemed like hours, but it was only minutes before Cal woke, groggy, to see Kris standing over him; he attempted to get up but felt a sharp blow to his head. He struggled to regain his faculties but found his hands and feet were bound with Kris dragging him out into the snow. He asked her what she was doing and why, but she said nothing. She stopped in an opening in the field about a hundred yards or so from the hut. Kris, laughing now, kicked him in the head and then staked his hands to the ground. Stunned but awake, he yelled to her as she walked away. Somehow the insane had become reality, Vitus' story, the nurse, the doctor, rabies, was he going to die? He called frantically to Kris, but she was gone.

Looking up at the blood red sky he heard what sounded like a dog panting. Light footsteps in the snow, Miska, he wondered. A shadow appeared in front of him and then hovered over him, the figure came right on top of him. He could only raise his head slightly, but it was unmistakable, a wolf. He was close enough to smell his breath and see his teeth. Cal worked his hands loose from the stake, knowing it was his only chance. As the wolf lunged at him, Cal swung, wildly connecting on the top of his head, then he pushed the wolf off with his hands still tied together and managed to get to his feet. With the beast's teeth firmly planted in between his tied hands, he kicked the wolf in the chest with everything he had. The wolf let go, Cal then swung again, grazing the tip of his nose. The wolf seemed stunned. Cal knew he had to act fast; he began screaming and swinging wildly, just hoping to survive. The wolf retreated into the woods, but this was not over, Cal got his hands and feet free when he could hear the sound of many footsteps. Like a stampede of canines. Light but with numbers, it sounded like thunder. The pack, it had to be the pack. Living in a real, live nightmare, everything he heard today was like prophecy. Funny how the absurd can become so real, so fast. What of Kris, is she sick, dead, rabies, mad. He had to get back to the hut quickly. As he approached the door, he cautiously opened it without a sound and took out his knife. Breathing heavy and still groggy, his eyes surveyed the dark hut for signs of Kris. A small candle lit in the center of the room gave the only light. The sound of the pack was getting louder as if they were growing in numbers. He whispered for Kris' his eyes found her sitting in the corner, not making a sound. He grabbed the candle and walked towards her; she rose, naked, covered in blood. Miska's body was laying in front of her, his insides ripped apart. Before he could speak, she lashed out at him, saying that he ruined everything, he's not coming back, he's not coming back. Cal asked who, but was interrupted by Kris telling him she would rather die than submit; she rushed past him out into the freezing cold night. Cal pursued but she was way too fast for him, an athlete himself, tonight he was not able run down his young wife. She disappeared into thin air. Alone now, out of breath and struggling to process everything, he heard the sound of the pack again. Louder and louder, but with Kris out there alone, did he continue to try to find her or save himself? He called out one last time as he turned towards the hut, and only took a couple of steps before confronting the same large, black wolf that almost killed him earlier. Standing perfectly still, the wolf moved closer with his glowing gold eyes piercing through the mist of the night. Cal's heart was pounding as if it wanted to leave his body. Showing his teeth and his intentions, the wolf lunged at Cal, tearing through his coat and down to his flesh. The blood dripped on the fresh snow. Shaken but still on his feet, Cal reached for his knife and awaited the wolf's next move. He obliged with a second strike, but this time Cal was ready, and as the beast exposed his chest, he drove the knife deep, twisting and turning. The weight of the beast forced Cal backwards onto his back, but he turned over the wolf and laid his full body weight on the knife handle. Still moving and biting at Cal, the wolf took hold of his arm, but with little fight left in him and Cal on top, the blade did its work, and soon the wolf stopped moving. As he realized what he had done and knew he was alive, Cal began crying out loud like a child. This was the first thing he ever killed, all the events of this evening led up to this moment, call it catharsis, but he knelt over the dead wolf and begged him for forgiveness. He forced himself to his feet and wiped his face dry of tears, then noticed someone walking towards him. He was shocked to see Kris, still alive, still naked and still covered in blood. He remembered what Vitus said about the blood of the Omega and ran to her. She slumped to her knees, and he noticed a hole in her shoulder, a bullet hole. He took off his coat to cover her and picked her up. As he walked towards his hut, men approached. Cal kept walking towards the men as they were walking towards him. He didn't look at them, didn't notice how many. One man stepped away from the rest and told him to stop. He kept walking. He raised his gun at Cal and demanded he stop. Cal kept walking. The man fired a warning shot into the air. Cal stopped as the man spoke he said the girl was sick and it had to be done. He said, "If you don't stop, we will shoot you.: Cal never spoke; he just continued walking to his hut. Maybe he had faced his destiny or just wasn't afraid to die anymore. He walked past the men on to his hut. They put down their weapons. Once inside the hut, he laid Kris down on the bed; she was all but gone. He grabbed her hand, told her he loved her, and she was not alone. She squeezed his hand and then went limp. Cal took blood from his arm and made a cross on her forehead, knelt down, and cried over her dead body. The noises in his head went silent, as if the world had stopped for a minute. All he could hear was his own heart, until one howl, then another, then another. The pack, right outside his door. He rose to his feet and summoned the last of his physical strength. To face his demons, it was either him or them. He opened the door and stepped into the cold night with the blood moon shining bright. The men he had encountered earlier were standing in front of him with rifles raised. One man stepped forward again; he said he was sorry, and this time he used Cal's name. He said this was not their choice. He asked if she were dead. Cal said nothing. He asked if

Cal were bitten. Cal said nothing. He was ready. They fired all at once. Cal fell to his knees and then face down in the fresh snow. His blood painted the ground. Inside the hut, Kris twitched and then opened her eyes.

Listen to the trees and you will hear
The sound of men becoming what they fear.
Prophecy consumed by the years
We search tirelessly for the truth
The end could be coming all too soon
Heed the warning of the Blood Wolf Moon

The Choice

Janet woke to a disturbing sound; her husband was having a terrible dream. She poked him, nothing, shook him, nothing. It was apparent this was no ordinary dream but a nightmare, complete with body shakes and mumbling. Because he slept on his side, facing opposite her, she had to sit up in bed and pull him over to his back. She spoke softly at first, then a little louder, using his name to break the spell this horrible dream had on him. He was trembling, near tears when he jumped up, asking the whereabouts of his three boys. Janet was confused, disoriented, and a little shaken herself; she was a cancer patient and heavily medicated to relieve the pain. "Is this about the nightmare?" she asked. "Do you want to talk about it? she added. He said no, but there was something in his voice that alarmed his wife. "Okay, what is it?" she said. Herman worked two jobs; Janet worked too, but with three boys, a huge mortgage, car payments, insurance, and everything else, they barely made ends meet. Herman was a fabricator by trade, a part-time bartender, and in his little spare time, he wrote short stories, poetry, and a novel that he has been working on for years. He firmly believed if he could get published, all their financial worries would be over, or so he needed to believe. Janet sold used cars at a local car dealer; she never made much but every little bit counted. She knew her husband and he wasn't going to volunteer the information, so she asked again, what this was all about. He hesitated, trying to find the right words, knowing the question was insane. He sat, turned on the light on the nightstand, and told his wife he loved all three boys the same, but if he had to choose, absolutely had to choose. Janet was equally scared and annoyed at her husband to this point, not to mention she was still very weak from her bout with cancer. She asked him why anyone would have to choose, reminding him that it was just a dream.

(FLASHBACK)

Herman was always in a hurry these days, what with his wife bedridden on most occasions. In addition to being in a hurry and in a bad mood, he seemed to always be yelling at his oldest son. On this particular day, he needed John, his oldest, to occupy the two younger boys while he got some things done. As is the case with most teenagers, John was rebelling against almost everything, but especially his stressed-out father. The battle waged on today as Herman tried to do three things at once. He asked John again to entertain his younger siblings and John responded with his usual attitude. "I have no life because of these two rugrats," said John. "You have no life, huh, I wish I had your life," scoffed Herman. "I have to finish this paragraph, get dressed for the bar, pick up your mother's medicine, come back here with your grandmother to watch you guys, and then listen to bullshit from every unemployed alcoholic in Indiana County," he says. "I'll trade you any day of the week, son, now change the channel for Jake and get Jimmy a cup of pudding and keep them busy for a half an hour, if it's not too much trouble," Herman said sarcastically. His focus completely broken, he slammed his fist on the computer table with a simultaneous shit, shit, shit, and yelled that he was leaving to get the medicine. He got into his old mini-van and headed to the drugstore for Janet's prescription, wondering what would happen if he just drove this piece of shit out of the state and kept going. He thought he could head south and keep going 'til he hit the ocean, get a job, find a place, maybe a dog, and screw this life. As he was thinking this, he pictured his life without his wife and kids, and wondered if it would have any meaning. He got married to his childhood sweetheart right after high school; of course; her pregnancy sped up the process and maybe kept him from college, but he never blamed Janet. If anything, he blamed himself. Janet was hot and Herman was not; she could have married better. Herman was not popular; Janet was warm, friendly, and everybody loved her. If Janet would have gone away to college, she would have met someone and never came back to Blairsville. A thought that had never escaped Herman's attention, along with the fact that if he hadn't gotten her pregnant, they probably wouldn't have married. So he got a job and bought a little house where they had John and Jimmy. When Janet was pregnant with Jake, they had to sell the small, two-bedroom ranch and get a large, three-bedroom with a yard and a hefty mortgage. If everything went well, they were fine, that was if Herman got forty hours at the granite shop, weekends at the bar, and Janet sold a car. Right now, Herman was laid off from the granite shop and Janet hadn't worked for six months; she was quite ill with ovarian cancer. Herman picked up the prescription and Grandma, then headed back to the house. Upon entering the house, he heard screaming, all three televisions blaring, Jake was half-naked, covered in chocolate, and John was on his phone. Herman looked at his mother-in-law and she knew he was ready to blow. "I'll take care of this, you better get to work," she said. "Before I go, I have to have a word with John," he said. "Okay, but remember, he is just a boy," she said. "John, get off that frickin' phone and come with me," he said. They stepped into the bedroom and Herman shut the door. "Give me the phone," he said. "What?" said John. "Give me that damn phone,"

Herman yelled. He grabbed it and ripped the flip top off its hinges, and pieces fell to the floor. "What, why did you do that?" asked a stunned John. "When I left here, I told you to watch your brothers and stay off that phone," he said angrily. John tried to explain, but his father was very angry. "Son, I asked you to do one thing and..." he said. He paused, but John stepped in here, almost as if he were waiting for this moment. "You always say one thing, but it is never one thing, it's always... everything," said John. "I come straight home from school every day and immediately start to do your job," he continued. "My job, you ungrateful little shit, my job is making money, and when I ask you to help, all you give me is selfish back talk," said Herman. "Your mother is on her death bed, and I am holding everything together, so if I ask you to watch your brothers, do it," he shouted. "Death bed?" asked a shocked John. John's lips were quivering as he asked his father if his mother were going to be alright. Herman knew he had crossed the line here by saying that, but he was tired and stressed out, and saw this as an opportunity to get his son to do what he wanted. He continued with the dramatics, all the while watching his son's expression as he grew more and more afraid. He could have gone further, but the look on John's face told him that he had won this round. "Now I have to go to work, help your grandma clean up and then go to bed," he said. "Bed? It's seven o'clock," said a still-shaken John. "Yeah, you're grounded too," said Herman. "This is just not fair," said John. "Fair, fair, you don't have a clue what fair is," said Herman. He slammed the bedroom door behind him as he headed out to the front door. His mother-in-law met him with an angry look on her face. "How could you tell that boy his mother is dying?" she asked sternly. "I don't have time for this right NOW," said Herman. "He is fifteen and doing the best he can with a terrible situation, you need to remember he is a child," said Grandma. "He needs to grow up fast and face the reality of this, if I had someone telling me the things I tell him, my life would have turned out..." said Herman. "Turned out, what, better?" asked Grandma. "Yes, better, better financially, materially, better all the way around," snapped Herman. "You may never have a lot of money, but you are certainly rich," snapped Grandma. "I lost my husband, Janet's father, when she was a baby, and no amount of money could ever give me what he did while he was here," she said. "In fact, I would have given any amount of money, any and all possessions, and lived in a cardboard box to have him back," she said. "We don't get to make those choices, but if you believe she is dying, then she is, if you tell your son she is dying... then she is... and if you don't love that boy for who is and who he can be rather than hating him because he reminds you of you, then you have just sentenced yourself to a fate worse than death," said Grandma. Herman rolled his eyes and slammed the front door behind him.

He pulled into the parking lot of the sleazy little bar where he would spend the next seven or eight hours of the night, and sat in his car for a second to collect his thoughts. Remembering what his mother-in-law said to him only moments ago still resonated in his head. He scoffed over the "a fate worse than death" remark. Getting out of his car and walking in the back door, he hoped it was not busy tonight. Once inside, he saw that it is dead and wanted it to stay that way. Herman wasn't much of a people person these days with all that was going on in his life. He always felt he was meant for something better than the small town of Blairsville had to offer. Raised by hard-working people who believed in jobs as necessary but not much on education. He even made up a slogan for their attitude; it went like this:

"college is for those other guys; I want the life ten dollars an hour buys." In high school, he was a good athlete, had musical and artistic talents, but without the support of his family, he never got the chance to pursue any of those interests. He has carried that grudge with him all his adult life, as well as the notion that when his family found out that Janet was pregnant, they knew he would never leave Blairsville and have to find a middleclass job. An axe he grinded on a daily basis. He always felt out of place in Blairsville, a red-neck little town with predominantly blue-collar jobs, high unemployment, and drug use. Most of Herman's high school buddies left town for college and never came back. He had work friends and family, he had Janet's friends and her family, but he still felt empty.

When the bar was busy, the time flew by, but when it was slow, he could think about his writing, or his wife; however, to-night his son took center stage in his mind. The locals were present and accounted for with a sprinkling of losers and drug users. He painted on his fake smile and got ready to walk the long mile. It was an easy night as Herman went back and forth in his mind over his encounter with his oldest son; he could hear his father saying things like that to him, which was the cause for most of his resentment. John had no ambition and cared little about anything, but he was only fifteen, neither did he at that age. If he were hard on John, would he respond or would he just make the wrong decisions out of resentment as well? His parents could afford to send him to college, but it was never even discussed. He wondered if he could afford to send his boys to college, and if he could, would they go? There was a junior college, the military and trade schools. If John were left to his own vices, he would do nothing and be nothing. The more he thought about the situation, the more it gave credibility to his position;

the validation would be essential for the inevitable round two when he got home. At least this little problem kept his mind occupied so as to not think about Janet tonight. It was time to clean up and get last call, this crowd was dead, and he was done. He ended every shift with, "Last call, money on the bar, and get to your car." A voice came from the end of the bar responding to his clever words. A man he didn't know recognize told him he should try writing. "Tonight, I am a bartender, a tired bartender," says Herman. "Ever think about writing?" the man asked. Herman moved closer to get a look at the man he ignored for most the night as he picked up the measly tips scattered on the bar. He acknowledged the patrons going out the door and addressed the last person in the bar. "One for the road?" he asked. "Sure," he said. "Another draft?" asked Herman. "Whiskey, neat," said the man. "I'm a writer, among other things," he added. Herman was immune to the bullshit he heard in a bar and knew the clientele he served were all delusional, so he nodded a lot and said, really a lot. "I know what you're thinking, what a lot of bullshit, right?" said the man. "You've heard it all, right?" he added. "I wrote this story about a man, like you, working hard to make ends meet, kids, mortgage, struggling... sound familiar?" he asked "Two jobs, studying for a masters or writing the great American novel, that's you, right?" he added. Herman continued to clean up while listening; he added a nod and a "Really?" "How is your wife, Janet, right?" he asked. This got Herman's attention because he didn't know this man. "How do you know my wife?" he asked. The man ignored the question and asked another. "What stage is her cancer?" he asked Herman became visibly annoyed with the invasion of his privacy. "I'll bet there are times when you wish you could wave a magic wand and make all of your troubles disappear, all of your dreams come true," the man said. "Yeah, don't we all, but seriously, I am going to lock up now," said Herman. "My story has a happy ending and so can yours, what if someone gave you a choice, made you a deal?" he asked. "Take away the pain, the worry, the stress, have the job you want, live where you want with the person you want, would you listen?" he asked. Herman was getting angry and just wanted the man to leave, peacefully. "Everyone has a secret wish, a dream or an escape from the life they have created for themselves," said the man. "It's all in how you look at it, most people are just as afraid of the life they want as they are the life they have," he continued. "Most people are afraid to make the tough choices, leave your wife because she is sick and is never going to get better, give up on my kids because I see what and who they will become, sell my house that I can't afford and live where I can," he said. Herman was pissed now. "Okay pal, that drink is on me, now get the hell out, you don't have to go home but you got to get the hell out of here," he said sternly, "Hell, huh, that's funny, I am going, my friend, but before I do, I want you to think about this," he said. "You have already made the choices in your mind, and you know how they will turn out," he said. "What is holding you back is the fact that the people that care about you need you to live this way, the people that you care about need you to live this way," he said. "Your whole life is need, your own happiness is tied to what other people need, you think these people won't love you anymore if you're happy, you can't love yourself if they are not happy... and that's why you're miserable," he added. Herman was pushing the man out the door but listening to every word. "What was the name of your story, I really did wish in one hand and shit in the other?" he asked. Just as the man opened the door to leave, he turned to say one last thing to Herman, and when he did, his eyes became frightening. "You know you would make the choice if given the opportunity, living with it is what is hard," he said.

The drive to and from the bar was only fifteen minutes but the time was priceless, a chance to get away from the pressures and relax with the only responsibility, keeping the car on the road. He listened to music as loudly as he wanted or just sat in peace and took stock of his life. Often, he would compose himself for the next phase of his endless drudgery. Tonight, he couldn't help but rehash the conversation he had with the strange man. He loved his family, but Janet was sick and showed no signs of getting better; actually, the prognosis was dire. He loved his boys, but John was surely to end up just like him and that was a constant source of aggravation. Jimmy, the middle child, was eight and he was just like Janet, smart, personable, handsome, everybody loved him, and then there was Jake, the youngest. He was a surprise, Herman and Janet were not really trying, but nonetheless, he came along three years ago, and he was a delight. A beautiful baby that grew into a beautiful child, never a problem, loved life, and Herman could not imagine his life without little Jake. Actually, even on his worst days, the one thing that kept him going was knowing little Jake was waiting for him to come home and play superheroes with him. Little Jake, Herman lovingly referred to him as "the reason" and never told anyone why. As he pulled into his driveway, his mood suddenly changed, he knew Janet would be awake and angry with him for what he said to John. He knew he would have to hear about how he handled the situation and how rude he was to Grandma. Fumbling with the keys and mumbling to himself, his cell phone rang, it was his home phone. "Hello, yeah, I am right outside the door," he said. Opening the door, he realized that something was very wrong. "I called 911, Janet is seizing," said Grandma. "Okay, I'll ride with her in the ambulance, you stay here with the kids," said Herman. "John is up and he wants to be with his mother," said Grandma. "No, he's ground..." (Before he finished the word, he realized he was being an ass.) "Get in the car, John, can you stay here?" he asked Grandma. "Of course, we will catch up to you later, everything is going to be fine," she said. "Buckle up, John," said Herman. "You don't wear seat belt," said John. "It's always an argument with you, isn't it?" asked Herman? "What, do as I say, not as I do," asked John? "Fine, don't wear one, the choice is yours," said Herman. It was four in the morning and a heavy, wet snow was falling on the road; Herman was right on the back bumper of the ambulance.

"Better give the ambulance some room," said John. "Excuse me, but you don't even have a permit yet," said Herman. "So? I know you are going to kill Mom if that ambulance has to stop," said John. Herman was out of patience with his son and the ambulance; he pulled out around it and floored the gas pedal. "Are you crazy?" said John. "Watch your mouth, and yeah, maybe I am," said Herman. The rear tires spun on the wet road then caught on a dry spot, propelling the car like a torpedo. The visibility was poor, but Herman gave it more gas and cut the car over to the right lane when he saw the ambulance far in the rear view. He looked over at John, who was covering his eyes, and couldn't resist making fun of him. John noticed headlights in his peripheral as they crossed into an intersection; a coal truck was coming right at them and not stopping. "Dad, look out!"

Herman woke from a quick jerk of his arms, as if he were falling in his dream. Often, he woke up swearing, shit, shit, shit, not knowing where he was or how he got there. Janet entered the room to inform him of her plans to pick the boys up at practice. She knew from the look on his face that he had nodded off and had no idea where he was or what had happened. It was the result of the accident; on occasion when he fell asleep, he woke with no memory of the past. Short term memory loss, a real life *50 First Dates* thing. Janet would have to calm him down and walk him through the events that has shaped their lives to this point. It was painful for her to have to relive the experience on a regular basis, but it was necessary and she remembered how Herman cared for her while she dealt with cancer. "Okay, Herman, Herman, stay with me here," she said. Not remembering anything, he asked her why she was out of bed. Janet always answered the same, stating she was fine, no more cancer. Herman then asked where his boys were and if John did what he was told to do. Janet held back her tears and informed her husband again of her plans. "I am going to pick Jimmy up at football and Jake from soccer, your parents are coming over for supper that my mother is making," she said. She put on a hard smile and reminded him that he was a best-selling author, they lived in southern California, and she would be right back. Just as she turned to exit, he asked about John again. She took a deep breath and explained that John was with God, she would be back in a half an hour, and told him to go outside and get some fresh air. Herman was still confused and not at all satisfied with the answers his wife had provided. He looks around the room at books he has no recollection of writing. Pictures of his family, Janet, Jimmy, and Jake, his mother and father. In the middle of the bookshelf was a hardback book that stood alone. He walked over, picked it up, and opened the jacket; inside was a handwritten dedication to his son, John. He didn't remember writing the dedication or the poem that ended the dedication. He read it out loud: *My first-born son is turning eleven, his time here will build my stairway to Heaven. One step at a time, securely in place. I stand on one then another to test for weight. He holds my hand but stays one step behind. It's so hard to tell him how much he changed my life.* Herman began to tremble but turned the page and started to read the first couple pages of the book entitled *The Choice.* It told the story of a man who struggled with life and the choices he had made. Marrying his childhood sweetheart after she became pregnant, struggling financially every day, and the bitterness that ensued. His wife became very ill with cancer and was given little chance to live. He had three boys, a huge mortgage, and no future. One night, he met a strange man at a bar where he worked part-time. The man convinced him that he had choices and could have everything he wanted if he just made the tough decision. A chill goes down his back as he reads further. The strange man offers the bartender a deal; his first-born son for the life he always wanted. Herman couldn't read anymore; he slammed the book down and left the room, looking for someone to give him answers. He found his mother-in-law in the kitchen preparing dinner. "Oh, you're up, I am making your favorite, lasagna," she said. "You want a drink before dinner?" she asked. Herman couldn't believe everyone was so happy and care-free, and his frustration got the best of him. He lashed out, demanding to know why everyone was so damn happy, why didn't anyone care? His mother-in-law was shocked and asked him what they should be caring about. Herman stuttered and stammered a bit, then shouted, "Where's JOHN?!" Grandma looked him in the eye with an evil look that reminded him of someone he met once. "This is what you wanted, isn't it?" she asked "What I wanted?" shouted Herman. "Yes, you wanted this and made the choice!" she snapped. "What choice, that was a book I wrote!" he snapped back. "You wrote that after the accident," answered Grandma. "Are you saying that I did this... on purpose? That I would give up my son for all of this? Where is he? This is some sort of sick joke... a lesson you are trying to teach me!" yelled Herman. He runs through the house randomly, yelling for his son to appear. Aimlessly shouting until a gut feeling made him go back into the study. On his computer was the same sentence written over and over. "What is holding you back is the fact that the people that you care about need you to live this way, the people that care about you need you to live this way." "Your whole life is need and your happiness is tied to that need." "You think these people won't love you anymore if you're happy and you can't love yourself if they are not happy." "That's why you are so miserable." "You have already made the choice in your mind, you just have to live with it now." Herman scrolled down the page, and this was all he could see, trying to erase it, but it kept coming back. He pulled the plug on the computer and the screen went black until a tiny light in the middle of the screen got bigger and bigger. It began to form words and he waited for it to become readable. It stopped and he read it: "He walks softly and carries a big heart; I wanted a family, and he was the best way to start. It's a hard journey from boy to man. I will be there to help as much as I can. He's already made tremendous strides. Sometimes we laugh... sometimes we cry. He has taught me to be both brave and kind. When adversity strikes as it does sometimes in life, I look in his eyes and see the man hidden inside. Wipe these tears from my eyes. Tears of joy... tears of pride." He picks up the computer and slams it to the ground.

"John, John, John... Where are you, John?" "Wake up, Herman, you were talking in your sleep again," says Janet. "Where are the boys, where's John?" he asked. "Sleeping, you can yell at John in the morning," she said. "It can't wait," said Herman. "Herman, leave it alone, I will talk to him about helping out more," she said. "No, I need to talk to him now," he said. "You don't need to say anything more, I heard that you told him I was dying, what the hell where you thinking?" snapped Janet. "I wasn't thinking, but I am now, and I see things very clearly, I know you are not dying, you will be fine," he said. "Because I said you are going to be fine you will be fine, I need to tell John something right now," he said. "What, that he needs to grow up, be more responsible, be stronger, what?" asked Janet. "No, not at all," said Herman. He entered the boys' bedroom to find Jimmy fast asleep, the light was on in the bathroom, and he could hear the boys trying to be quiet. John was trying to help his little brother pull up his pajamas. "Come on, Jake, I need to get some sleep," said John. "If you wake up Dad, that is my ass," he said. "Dad is awake," said Herman. John was bracing himself for one of his father's famous tongue lashings; instead he noticed a different look on his face, one he was not used to seeing. At this moment, he saw love, compassion and pride in his eyes. "Good job, John, you are a good brother and a hell of a son. We will need to get out today and get you a new cell phone," he said. "Your dad is a jerk sometimes. I love you, John," he added. John smiled for the first time in a long time and told his father he loved him too.

St. Samael

John Harrison's emotions ran the gambit as he approached the place where he once was regarded as a genius. The car he was riding in came to a stop in front of St. Samael, a hospital for the criminally insane. Gut-wrenching fear, panic, anxiety, regret, and embarrassment, especially embarrassment, ran on an endless loop. Michael Sands, his new friend and the new administrator, assured him that things would get better, easier. Ten years ago, John was the top psychiatrist in his field, pioneering methods of treatment for the most dangerous and depraved souls known to the western world. He was published, successful, well paid, and married to his childhood sweetheart. Ten years ago. Last night, he slept in his car. Michael gently put his hand on John's back as if to push him toward the front door and a fresh start to his life, as the night security guard. Michael promised John that he would do everything in his power to help him get his license back, but this first step was essential to the process. John was burned out, an addict, a loser who had given up, and just wanted to get a shower, shave, and maybe a hot meal. He wasn't interested in helping anyone including himself. This hospital represented everything he was running from, all the things that made him what he is today. Almost ten years ago to the day.

These days, St. Samael was the last resort for almost everyone. It wasn't always that way; in fact, it wasn't always called St. Samael. Once, it was the premier psychiatric hospital in the state, named after St. Samuel. The finest staff and accommodations could be found there, and John was the best in his field. Graduating at the top of his class at Harvard, he decided to turn down a cushy private practice for the chance to do something he called, "life changing." Working with criminals that often were in restraints for the remainder of their lives was, indeed, life changing. These criminals had a reputation for extreme violence, were openly belligerent, and could not be trusted without an armed guard. On occasion, some would actually achieve a kind of celebrity status through the newspapers that covered the crimes that led to their stay at St. Samuel. One such case was Darwin Morrow, a young man that was sexually abused by both of his foster parents from the time he was five. Around his fifteenth birthday, he beat them both to death with his bare hands. He then took a garden claw aerator, honed the ends to a razor's edge, and carved out the private parts of his foster parents. The next three years had him escaping from every juvenile detention home he was put in, and it is believed he was responsible for the death and mutilation of eight more people, all married couples, where one or both were convicted of sex crimes. He was dubbed the "X Mutilator" by the newspapers because the police photos of the crime scene were so graphic that cardboard X's had to be placed over the mutilated parts in an attempt to censor the horror from the public eye. An anonymous tip led the police to Darwin, living under a bridge, but he was declared unfit for trial. John was intrigued by Darwin and that brought him to St. Samuel. He had pioneered an innovative approach to the criminally insane which included the use of a new experimental drug. John believed that these deeply disturbed patients' brains were producing a chemical that shut down normal function, thus leaving them with little or no reasoning power, no compassion, and illusions of living in a world of their own creation. Working with scientists and chemists, John helped to develop a drug that calmed the patients, brought back reasoning, compassion, and reality, jokingly referred to as "A dose of reality." The drug was used only at St. Samuel under John's supervision, and it was considered a success for the less violent patients. Darwin was the inspiration for the drug; he was always heavily sedated and never without restraints, for everyone's safety as well as his own. The same day he was committed, he found a razor blade and cut off his own lips. It was John's idea for him to wear a surgical mask to hide the disfigurement; he and Darwin had sessions every day with little or no results. Darwin had withdrawn completely and that was what bothered John the most. He was the best at his job because he took every case personally, even though his wife of five years and childhood sweetheart would say he took them too personally. He and Greta, his childhood sweetheart and wife, were trying to start a family despite John's busy schedule, which often took him out of town on speaking engagements. Darwin became an obsession for John, always the optimist, always pushing the envelope, he wanted to try a radical treatment. It had been standard practice with less disturbed patients to take them back to the place or circumstance that was believed to be the breaking point. At this point, under his supervision, John would allow the patient to go through the "four R's:" remember, relive, restructure, rebirth. This procedure bad a ninety-percent success rate. If this idea were promoted by anyone other than John, the hospital would have declined, but given his status in his field, he was given a long leash. Despite his pension for violence, John felt that Darwin had a gentle soul, and only after years of humiliation and abuse did he create this evil persona for his own preservation. John intended to take him back to where he became the "X Mutilator" and find the young man named Darwin Morrow. Hands and feet shackled and accom-

panied by three armed guards, John and Darwin made the journey back to his beginning.

Darwin never looked up; instead, he fumbled nervously
with his fingers as the car he rode in pulled up in front of the
abandoned house where grew up. John was nervous as well but
didn't want Darwin to pick up on it, so he tried to engage him
in simple conversation before they proceeded to the house. The
next step proved to be the most critical in this process as John
believed the house represented a mental and emotional prison
for his patient. Darwin never looked up, he ceased fumbling
with his fingers, his body language suggested calmness, and that
was a sign that John came to understand as he had made a decision. One guard stayed outside the front door, one went to the
backdoor, and one accompanied John and Darwin into the
house. The house wreaked of mold, decay, and death, not sur-
prising since it had been empty after the brutal murders. John
looked around the room quickly and then turned his undivided
attention to his patient, expecting some physical reaction to the
place where Darwin became the X Mutilator. He engaged in
more small talk conversation with the guard, hoping to be a dis-
traction, all the while watching his patient's body language.
Ninety percent of patients whom John had exposed to this
procedure experience the four R's; unfortunately Darwin was
in the ten percent. Disappointed but never deterred, John decided it was enough for today. He turned to take one last look
at this house of horrors when he felt a sharp pain on the back of
his head, and everything went black. The time it took for him
to wake up in the hospital and focus on where he was, what had
happened, was probably longer in his mind than actual time
elapsed. Often, people who black out, for whatever reason, wake
up shouting obscenities. John woke up and immediately asked

about Darwin. His heart raced as if he knew something terrible had happened. The police were outside his door, waiting to talk with him; he sunk down in his bed and wept like a child as the whole story unfolded before him. Darwin had killed all three guards, escaped, and... John could not stay conscious as the police told him his wife had been slaughtered.

The irony of walking the halls in the very hospital that provided both fame and fortune, and the impetus for the disintegration of his life, was not lost on a man who took an oath to study the mind. He could feel the memories fighting their way into his head, fighting through the past ten years of alcohol and drug abuse. He opened a flask of cheap bourbon whiskey and took a big gulp, while pictures and images flashed like an old-time camera. He knew he would not make it through the night unless he got a little help, and an insane asylum had to stock a number of anti-psychotics, anti-depressants, and assorted pain killers. The only trick was getting past the night nurse, who, if memory served, would be the only one here with the key to the pharmaceutical room. Johns' social skills had eroded to the point that he just avoided any human contact, so as he crept around each corner, he expected to have to engage in enough small talk to reach his destination. All was quiet, too quiet; in fact, there was no one to be found, no nurse, no janitor, no patients. Odd, very odd. Standing in front of the locked door to the pharmacy, he contemplated how to get into the room without a key. Like any junkie, John only thought of the end result, getting numb as fast as possible. However, he didn't want to make noise that would bring someone's attention, so he took off his jacket and began pushing on the glass, which was reenforced with a wire mesh, but one thing at a time. He had little physical strength left and only the desire to alter his mind gave him enough inspiration to continue with this painful task. He started to come to the conclusion that the room was tamper-proof considering the type of patients that it contained. John gave it one last push when he noticed a figure behind him from the reflection in the glass. He instantly went into denial mode, expecting it to be the night nurse, but turned to see a young girl in patient garb that was soaked with blood. She was incoherent and babbling, and John's instincts were to run since that was all he did for the past ten years. She reached out and grabbed his arm, babbling on about the devil and what he did to her, lifting up her gown to reveal a strange symbol burned into her mid-section. He only needed one night, all the drugs he could smuggle, a few bucks, and he was back on the street, but the price was too high. As he wrenched the girl's hands off of him, the elevator from the basement stopped, the doors opened, and the girl vanished. John had a reason for being there now and the opportunist in him stayed to see if he could benefit from the encounter. He was surprised to see his new friend and boss, Michael, exit the elevator. As John stumbled over his words explaining the situation, Michael seemed distracted and only wanted to know how he liked his first night on the job. They walked and talked with Michael's hand on John's back, gently directing him back to the elevator. "I want to show you something," said Michael. They got out in the basement; John began to feel the presence of something unexplainable. If he were going to be fired, it wasn't going to happen in the basement. John asked Michael where they were going, feeling like a child who had done something wrong, and was about to be admonished. Michael opened the door to the boiler room; John reluctantly followed. Moving some debris that concealed a trap door in the floor, he explained how the hospital was built over a temple that existed hundreds of years ago. "You have to see this," said Michael. A dim light in the distance was the only reference point, so John fixed on it as Michael's voice guided him in the dark. Just a little further was the last thing he heard.

Often when people black out, for whatever reason, they wake up shouting obscenities. John's head hurt and he was disappointed that whatever hit him didn't deliver the blow that ended his life. As he fully regained consciousness, he realized his hands were bound above his head and anchored to the wall. Looking around the room that held him captive, his eyes began to focus on several things at once. The table in the center of the room, strange looking symbols drawn in red all over the floor and candles hung on the walls providing the only light. It smelled of death. Suddenly the door opened, and John heard a voice say, "You don't remember me, do you?" It was Michael. "My head hurts really badly, but I remember you," said John. "Well, I'm the one that gave you the headache, both of them, but that's not what I meant," said Michael." What do you mean, both of them?" said John. Michael interrupted by showing John a picture of the hospital staff taken ten or eleven years ago. John acknowledged the picture but was puzzled by the significance, "That's me with the hair and the beard, I was an orderly here when you came to our humble abode," said Michael. "An orderly," said John? "Yes, we met, but I am sure you were just too important to remember a lowly orderly," answered Michael. "How does an orderly become hospital administrator?" asked John. That is the power of Satan," said Michael. John knew this conversation was heading in a deadly direction, so he asked again what Michael meant by both headaches. Michael explained how he hid in the old, abandoned house, waiting for the opportunity to set Darwin free. "I cold-cocked you, I killed all three guards knowing Darwin would get the blame, and I led him to your house," he said. Michael had John's full attention now. "You see, while I was working here, Darwin and I developed a rapport, all of your bullshit education and mind-altering drugs couldn't get through, but I did," he said. "The power of Satan, you couldn't even get him to speak, I convinced him to cut off his own lips, the power of Satan," said Michael. "You tried to make him into a normal human being, I embraced the savage in him and let him loose on the world to do Satan's bidding," he continued. "I unleashed the beast, the perfect killing machine, and told him to do what he does best, I led him to your house so he could slaughter your pregnant wife, carved out her breasts and genitalia as an offering to Samael," he said. "Pregnant?" said a shocked John. Michael paused, surprised that John didn't know his wife was expecting their first child. "You see, Darwin has been a soldier in Satan's army since you arrived here ten years ago," said Michael. John was beginning to see the pieces of the puzzle come together when the door to the room opened again and in walked Darwin. Michael flipped a switch on the wall that shed a brighter light on the room, Darwin looked much the same, the white surgical mask that covered his hideous mouth was almost black, and his hair had not been washed or cut in years. His body language was still that of someone ashamed of who and what he had become. His eyes never reached John's but somehow, silently they acknowledged each other.

In his hands, Darwin held two jars, even from across the room, John knew what they contained. "Well done, you have served our master well and he is pleased," said Michael. Michael had taken on a disturbing new persona, one of arrogance and megalomania. He was shamelessly gloating while he took credit for the unraveling of John's life. John interrupted the sermon long enough to ask if Michael were the master mind behind some plot to create a race of serial killers? "Close, very close, but I think years of cheap booze and drugs have clouded your powers of perception," said Michael. The therapist in John forced him to bring Michael down to Earth by explaining that he coerced a young man who had a history being coerced by authority figures. He used information that was private and confidential to get Darwin to do himself and others harm. Michael was listening now with a slight smirk on his face. John continued to lecture by stating that Michael took a boy who killed once in an effort to eradicate the terrible things that were done to him and turned him into a mindless, soulless creature of destruction. "All in the name of Satan," said Michael. "But my wife, why? She was innocent," said John. Michael explained that he needed to destroy John first, so that he then he could be reborn. He went on to say, "It has been determined that you are to lose all of your earthly possessions, die here, and then be summoned back as Marduk, the magician." Michael drew the seal in the dirt that would be burned into John's flesh. It was similar to the one he saw on the hysterical girl earlier. Michael continued, stating that John's wife would be waiting on the other side of the gate of Nanna. "There you will be reunited with her as you both return to this world." "To do your bidding?" asked John sarcastically. "No Idimmuu, the destroyers. Idimmt serves Cthulhu, but all of that can wait," said Michael. "So destroying my life and running the hospital into the ground was all some bizarre scheme?" said John. "Plan, not scheme, and I wouldn't say bizarre," said Michael. "How did you get hired as administrator?" asked John. "I never said I was an administrator, you simply assumed," answered Michael. "But what about the staff, the patients, the janitor?" asked John. "No staff, no janitor, and no patients, all disciples waiting for their own transformation," said Michael. It suddenly dawned on John that the girl he saw earlier was a subject of one of these pagan rituals; she escaped before she could be sacrificed. "This temple has been the sight of human sacrifice for hundreds of years, there are tunnels leading from this very room to the streets," explained Michael. No one outside of this order had this information, even after the hospital was built right on top. The order expanded its numbers and the need for secrecy became a priority. The hospital provided adequate cover and a constant source for recruits, but with John's popularity came more attention, more scrutiny. Michael stopped there and turned his attention to Darwin and the two jars; he opened the jars and dumped the contents of both out on the table in the center of the room. He dipped his fingers in the bloody organs and drew a sign on the table. "Asarualim, possesses secret wisdom and shines light on the darkness, you will be witness to the power, the future," said Michael. He called the others in the room and John watched in horror as they consumed the organs. When finished, Darwin left the room and then entered a moment later with a lifeless body that John recognized as the girl from upstairs. Darwin threw her down on the table, reached under his dirty jacket, and pulled out the razor-sharp claw that earned him the name "X Mutilator." He raised it above his head and waited for Michael's approval. He was demonstrating the power he had over Darwin, the power of Satan, the power of Samael. He couldn't help gloating one more time. Michael finished by ordering Darwin to bring down the pain and he struck with such force that the girl's left breast was completely removed in one motion. John had turned away, but the sound was one he would not soon forget... if he lived. Desperate times brought out the best in some, and this certainly qualified as John reached deep into his memory, searching for something that would give him hope.

Two things John knew for certain about Darwin were that he was susceptible to influence from figures be deemed to have power over him, and he despised child molesters. Using this information, he channeled Darwin's father in his voice and demanded him to stop; to his astonishment it worked. "Darwin, you are a bad boy, you are going to be punished, and you know what that means," he said. "What are you doing?" asked Michael. "Don't listen to him, do what you are told!" he barked. Michael took out a vile of liquid that John assumed was "a dose of reality" intended for him; he had to act quickly. "Darwin, I am very disappointed in you, drop that thing and come here," yelled John. Darwin became irritated and confused. John could tell from his body language that he could snap at any moment. He had to push and hope for the best. "Darwin, this man here is going to teach you a lesson, now bend over and take down your pants!" shouted John. Michael had the shot ready and moved quickly towards John, but Darwin jumped in his way. Michael yelled, then screamed, then pleaded for Darwin to stop, but it was no use; once in motion, Darwin couldn't stop. John turned his head again but could see in the shadow on the wall, he could hear the bones break, and Michael's pleas died off into a faint whisper. Darwin stopped when Michael's body showed no life. He picked him up and threw him down on the table beside the girl, looking around for his claw so he could finish the job. John was still in a fight for his life. "Darwin, stop," he yelled. John knew he had a fifty-fifty chance of getting out of this alive, depending on what he said in the next minute. He was scared and his usually sharp thought process was failing him in his moment of greatest need. Michael was clearly insane and delusional, but there was some truth to his rantings and ravings. Asarualim, Idimmuu, and Cthulhu were names he recognized from a book he read in college, *The Necronomicon*. If Michael was using this book to influence Darwin, perhaps John could do the same. He was running out of time as Darwin was coming toward him fast. He cleared his head and pictured a page from the book, quoting the only thing he could remember. "No Evil Spirit, No Evil Demon, No Evil God, No Evil Fiend, No Hag Demon, No Filth-Eating Demon, No Offspring of the Demon, No evil in the world or under it, or over it or inside the world may seize me here." John winced as Darwin raised his hands; he couldn't watch but felt his chains pulled from the wall and his arms fell to his side. He didn't want to look in Darwin's eyes for fear of what he might see; he said nothing and stood completely still, looking at the ground. Silently, they acknowledged each other. Darwin turned and left the room. John found the key to his shackles in Michael's pocket and left the room. It was morning and the hospital was empty; John left through the front door. He had a long walk ahead of him, but there was nothing but time. He wondered if going back to school and getting a surgical degree would be a good idea? Maybe healing the body would be safer than healing the mind.

The Sound of Death

It's funny where the mind will go when you just let it wander. I bought this old farmhouse before I was married and riding my quad on the seventeen-acre spread is both a passion and great therapy. The house needed work, but there was enough room to raise a family and own dogs, my other passion. The land bordered a two-hundred acre farm that once was the largest dairy farm in the area; now it belonged to one of those weekend farmers from out of state. One of those rich guys who never farmed, never intended to farm, just liked the idea of owning a farm. His name was Joe from New York and that's what I called him, Joe from New York, more of a hunter than a farmer. Deer were abundant in this area, and Joe from New York was a gun-toting, republican red neck that loved deer meat. On occasion, my dogs and I would stray a little and end up on his property; he was fine with me but terrified of my dogs. I had four Rottweilers: Ceaser and Damien were my males, Cleo and Lorali my females. The five of us took this ride every chance we got; it started at the house and ended at the hunting shack on Joe's property, maybe an hour, but we were never in any hurry to get back. Getting back meant an empty house now that my wife and I were a little divorced. She was a people person, a social butterfly who could turn even the smallest gathering into a blockbuster party. When I met Jennifer, she had friends, she had plans, she had a future. I told her I would not try to change her; I did. I told her she would still have friends; she didn't. I told her I would fix up the house, have parties, and entertain; I didn't, we didn't. I am a social misfit; that's why I bought this house, raised dogs that most people find intimidating, and kept to myself. I met Jennifer, fell madly in love, and promised her everything; I just didn't keep my promise. I had little use for people, hated my job, didn't have a career or ambition. My dogs were the only living things around me not bothered by these qualities. I was always told that if you loved someone, you wanted them to be happy, and Jennifer wanted me to be happy. She gave me two wonderful children. Melissa, my oldest, was thirteen, and Ben, my boy, was ten. She had been patient and loving for thirteen years but she was miserable. One day, she told me it was over and went to live in the city where she could have the life that made her happy. I would have the kids this weekend, and that meant Saturday and Sunday at the mall or video store. It was Friday and I was home from work, time for a ride before dark. It's funny where the mind will go when you just let it wander.

It was a chilly, mid-October afternoon, the perfect weather for a ride. The dogs realized what was coming when I started the bike; they could barely wait for me. While I was married the dogs stayed in a pen, but now that I lived alone, at least through the week, they lived in the house with me. Rottweilers are intensely loyal and protective: they rarely left my side, a quality I found more and more soothing. I had worn down a path into the woods behind my house that led to the neighbor's farm. The October sky was clear on this Friday afternoon. It had rained the day before, the trees were still wet, and small puddles littered the path to the open field. My dogs had run ahead of me, but I could hear them barking in the distance. Rottweilers are not normally noisy dogs, so if they bark, you need to investigate. Usually, it's a deer or small wild animal that they are chasing or have tracked. In a pack, the predatory instincts take over and God help anything that would take them on. I could tell by the sound that they had something cornered. As I came over the next hill, I expected to see them circling an opossum or raccoon; at the bottom of the hill was New

York Joe's hunting shack. He used it mostly to drink beer, but he wasn't supposed to be here this weekend. The closer I got, I realized that my dogs were serious; whatever was in there, they wanted, badly. I shut off the quad and hollered to see if someone would respond. "Is anybody in there? Joe you in there?" I asked. No answer. I noticed that the door had an old screwdriver in the latch to keep it closed from the outside. I thought that was odd. I walked around the perimeter, and it didn't appear as though there were any openings that even the smallest animal could have gotten through. I hollered again and shook on the door. "Joe, did you pass out in there?" I shouted. My dogs had calmed to the point that if I opened the door, I could get in without them storming the place. As the door opened, the light from outside lit up the little shack and I could see someone on the dirt floor. My dogs pushed passed me and now I had to go in the shack. If I shut the door, I wouldn't be able to see, so I had to let the dogs sniff and lick this person. I had hoped it was Joe and he was passed out drunk. The dogs lost interest if it wasn't something to eat or moving; they cleared the area, and I noticed then that the person was staked to the ground. I got closer and saw that it was a young girl, and her mouth was taped.

Her eyes were closed. I thought she was dead. Her clothes were dirty and torn, and now I was getting a disturbing image in my head of what had happened here. I called my dogs and was about to get out of there when she opened her eyes and let out a muffled scream that sent shivers through out my body. Part of me wanted to close the door behind me and just let the police handle this, but for some reason I couldn't leave. I bent down to tell her that I wouldn't hurt her, and I was going to remove the tape from her mouth. She continued to scream. Instead, I cut her loose so she could see I wasn't there to harm her, she squirmed and fought me every step of the way. I cut the last piece of rope and she was free. I said, "There, now will you calm down?" She began to cry, and I could not understand what she was saying with the tape on her mouth. "Take that tape off so I can understand you," I said. Stumbling around the small room, I could hear a crackling sound as if she were stepping on things made of plastic. Upon further inspection, I could see a bunch of DVDs, and then I noticed camera equipment on the make-shift shelves. "What went on here?" I asked her. She was sobbing incoherently, and I felt like this was my time to go, I had done enough here. As I motioned to her that I was leaving, I heard the sound of a truck approaching. She became hysterical, coming at me, arms flailing. I pulled her arms down and ripped the tape off her mouth. The tip of her tongue had been cut off; she was spitting blood into my face, screaming a muffled, "No, no, no." The picture was clear now; the person or persons in this truck were responsible for this and they were coming back. My dogs were on the job and met the truck as it came into my view; it stopped dead about one hundred yards from the shack. I was hoping the dogs would scare them off and stayed in the shack for the moment. Peaking through the door, I noticed the driver revving the engine, trying to frighten the dogs. That didn't work. He inched forward. That didn't work; the dogs stayed in front of the truck, not letting it move far or fast. No one inside had the courage to get out, but they didn't back up either. I just realized that my quad was parked in view, so what we were witnessing here was an old-fashioned Mexican stand-off. The truck began inching forward and showed no signs of stopping. My dogs backed up; it was time to make our escape. My quad could carry two and the dogs would follow me, but would this truck follow too? I stepped out of the shack, trying not to look at the truck, but when they saw me, the driver laid on the horn. I started the quad and told the girl to get on the back and hold on. The driver floored it and my dogs scattered. I turned the quad around and headed for the woods with my four dogs ahead of me. The mid-October sun was just setting behind the hills and the path back to the house seemed endless. I felt every bump because I couldn't lift my body for the weight of the girl on the back. My dogs were probably already home. I began searching my memory for something, anything that I had heard or saw that could give me a clue as to what I was dealing with here. Unfortunately, I would rather watch Sportscenter on an endless loop than watch or listen to the news. As we left the woods and entered the open field that was my backyard, it seemed as though darkness had suddenly fallen. Pulling up to the back door I shut off the quad, I could hear the dogs out front, but my attention was on the girl and what to do now. I didn't know if she were in shock or just plain exhausted, but she showed little signs of life. I nudged her to let her know we were going in the house to call the police; she said something that sounded like, "Fast, fast, fast." I grabbed her by the arm and lifted her to her feet. Each step on my back porch got harder for her; as we reached the backdoor, she was about to fall. I got her inside and quickly put her in a chair. Knowing that talking was difficult, I gave her a piece of paper and a pencil so she could write her phone number down. I went to get the phone and told her I was calling the police first. She handed me the paper and said those words again that I now understood to be "Dad, Dad, Dad." She laid her head down on the kitchen table as I dialed 911. I could still hear my dogs, so I went to the front porch to see what they were doing. "911, what's your emergency?" "I need the state police at..." I paused, because in scanning the front yard, I noticed my truck's tires had been slashed, and when I turned towards the door, I noticed writing or something on the side of my house. "Hello, 911, what's your emergency?" "Yes, I need the police at 1347 Rt. 6 East Ligonier, I have a girl here..." I paused again because I didn't know her name. "Hold on a minute, I need to ask her. What's your name?" I asked. "Here write it down," I said. She did not respond. "Sir, I need you to stay calm, and on the line," the operator said. "I am calm, but I don't know the girl's name and..." It sounded like the operator hung up on me and no dial tone. The phone was dead. I wasn't so calm now; my mind was racing with possible options, all the while I was running through the house to see if anyone had been inside. Did I need batteries for my cordless phone? Should I get back on the quad and head for the main road? Should I ask this girl what she did and who these people were that did horrible things to her? I wanted to know but didn't, because what I saw so far painted an ugly picture in my mind. Would more information make the situation more frightening or less? I was talking to myself and making no sense. Okay, I made a decision: I wanted my dogs in the house. I went to the front door and hollered for them. As I did, I noticed lights coming down the road. The driveway to my house was off a two-lane black top that led to a dead end. My house was five hundred yards from the black top, and from my front porch, I could see any vehicle on that road. In the course of a year, you could count on one hand how many vehicles came down that road. They were either lost or coming to my house. They were coming to my house. For a split second I felt relief; it could be the police. My dogs ran into the house one by one. That split second of relief turned to terror as I realized by the sound that it was the truck that had chased us earlier. It was so hard to think clearly, but I had to resist the temptation to get on the quad, let my dogs run, and leave this girl behind. I could outrun the truck by myself to the woods, but not with the girl on the back.

The truck stopped at my front porch with the headlights shining on the door; the driver revved the engine. I picked the girl up and took her upstairs to my son's room. Damien, one of my male Rotts followed. Lorali, one of my females, followed Damien because she never wanted to miss anything. I told her she would be safe here with these two beasts; she was unresponsive. I closed the door behind me. As I came down the steps, I could hear a dog yelping and thought the worst, but both of my dogs were sitting by the front door. I peeked out the window and I could see three men. One of them stepped in front of the truck's lights and held up the dog, the one I heard yelping, I assumed. I couldn't make out what happened next; there wasn't enough light, but soon after, the man threw the dog on my front porch. The dog was not moving. This must have been an attempt to scare me by showing me what they would do to my dogs or me. I don't know what came over me next, but instead of many jumbled voices in my head, I only heard one, my daughter Melissa's, and if someone had hurt her the way they hurt this girl, I would die getting revenge. I opened the door and claimed my house and property before God. The echo of my own voice died down, and then there was silence and then break-ing glass. They had gone around to the back porch and were try-ing to get in the upstairs window where the girl was, where Damien and Lorali sat waiting. Rottweilers don't make much noise before they attack, but the look on their face is a dead give-away. They look into your soul with lifeless, doll-like eyes, inch-ing forward and bumping with their chest, much like a shark sizing up their prey. They lunge, seize, and pull down all in one motion, then they shake their heads, again much like a shark, tear-ing and ripping the flesh. By the time I got to the room, the girl was still sitting on the bed where I left her. One of the men was laying face down on the floor in a pool of blood, seizing ferociously, Damien and Lorali sitting on either side, looking up at me as if they needed my approval. I gave it to them, told the girl I would be back, and grabbed my son's little league bat. Heading back downstairs, I realized I left the front door wide open; as my feet hit the bottom step, I heard someone at the back door. Ceaser and Cleo ran by me for the back door, but I could hear someone at the front door. I came down the hall leading to the living room, brought the bat back, and swung at head level. The bat landed on something hard, and I heard a thump, followed by a thud. The sounds were coming fast, and my mind could not handle the direction, but Ceaser and Cleo must have had someone at the back-door. I decided to let them deal with that as I took a look at my work. A man lay on his back in my doorway, out cold. The back door slammed shut, Ceaser and Cleo joined me, a bloody shoe lay on my kitchen floor.

It's funny where your mind will go if you let it wander. I wanted to sell my house. I wanted to re-unite with my wife Jennifer, I wanted to get some duct tape and tie up this man on my floor. I wanted banana pancakes and I wanted to call my mom. I wanted... I saw lights coming down the road; they were coming to my house. I hollered up to the girl that it was over and the police were here. I went outside. I could see the lights on the top of the cars, two state troopers. They pulled in behind my truck, "She's all right, I have her," I said. The exact sequence of events that followed are unclear. A man in a suit got out of one of the police cars; he walked with purpose. I stayed on the porch because I had to warn them about my dogs and the condition of the girl. The man pulled a gun out of his jacket and fired; everything went quiet. A small puff of smoke followed the shot, it floated for what seemed like an eternity, my eyes were fixed on the cloud, it turned into Jennifer's face and she blew me a kiss. I could hear people talking as they stood over me. I hoped my dogs were okay. Funny where your mind will go when you just let it wander.

Revelations

Revelations: An uncovering, unveiling, a previous unknown fact in a dramatic way. Bringing to light that which had been previously hidden

The following pages are my personal Revelations

Loup-garou Moon: Loup-garou, French for wolf-man

The House on the hill: A home that only exists in memory and dream

Melancholy: Death through the eyes of the dead

Home without Walls: The endless pursuit of freedom

Tallahassee: Inspired by Woody Harrellsons character in Zombieland

"We are not to question why there is pain,
just listen for the thunder and prepare for the rain"

"With one hand we work towards the future,
with the other we hold onto the past
gathering seeds to sow
hoping what we build will last"

REVELATIONS

"I am the product of the present and the past,
navigating the less traveled path,
the fork in the road if you will,
one more chance to push the stone up the hill"

Melancholy

The mood in the room was curiously serene
I moved cautiously, sensitive to grief
I am sorry but he is very sick
say good-bye, he will not live
Faces looked oddly familiar, expressions vague
the air turns cold as people gather in the hallway
whispering in the shadows, hoping they don't have to stay

Wondering amid those with little time left
the diseased and cancerous
who would take their last breath
I moved silently, effortlessly among them
like a dream that continued from night on into the day
memories were embellished for pity's sake

Voices interrupt my thought, as it is time to go
family and friends put on their coats
want to follow but denied by a feeling pale and cold
cry out to God, seeking a reason for this
loved ones blow a last kiss
My breath is the only sound
until the slow beat of a heart began to pound
abruptly, the sound comes to an end
screams fill my head as I recognize the dead

I don't know if tomorrow the sun will shine
'til then I will follow the light in the sky
we are all given just enough time

looking into the face of death, on this day it was mine

I was not a good person but I knew how to be kind

I was not a man of wisdom but now and then I was right

I was not a man of vision but now I see the light

I was not a man of faith, but I searched for a sign

Tallahassee

Pieces of broken glass
the mirror won't lie
I'm afraid to ask
just look with closed eyes
I walk barefoot on the sharp edges
still unclear as to the message

What is this place
the walls cold and grey
no windows, painted over doorways
children laughing with no faces
As I move forward, downward, what's behind me fades
A whimpering dog needs rescued
I cradle him, whispering, bless you
a shrouded figure with no eyes
points at me, shouting lies

What is this place
the walls cold and grey
no windows, painted over doorways
He says, "you must go down to get out,
and the puppy stays with me"
I care more for the puppy
than I do for me
if he were leading me to die
at least the puppy will be alive
as I descend
black water forms puddles on the floor

this must be the end
a voice not my own
says look to the sky,
let the light bring you home
God help me, I want my puppy
he said," listen to me,
you never had a puppy
you had a son
he's gone
there was an accident, with a gun"

The House on the Hill

The season passes with the cool wind of autumn
The smell feels like her pretty head resting upon him
Orange and brown falling all around
beads of sweat welcome the chill
silent and empty is the house on the hill

A place to call home can't fill an empty heart
the night won't let me touch the brightest star
time is just what passes by the window
like footprints on a fresh snow
that seem to have nowhere to go

Silence is the sound of wishing and hoping
hoping everything we had wasn't still broken
silent and empty is my heart until...
silent and empty is the house on the hill

White turns brown and white again
as promise withers to an end
The house looks so far away now
at times, when looking in, I see myself looking out
The memory is nothing more than a dim light
flickering like a candle in my mind
silent and empty is my heart until...
silent and empty is the house on the hill

Loup-garou Moon

Nary a man brave of heart
walks alone
on a night with one star
unto the madness it is to swoon
ravaged by the Loup-garou moon

Maliciously he crept
silently I wept
he takes back the night
like a fungus that grows on the rye
ergot, feasting parasite

Heart and soul bereft
ripping, tearing at my flesh
to my lord I plead for death
stop this malevolent force
reverse the theriomorph
blood stains on his teeth
limbs lay at his feet
the beast has no compassion
the act is its own contrition
the body falls to the ground
the beast's howl is the only sound
spitting out pieces of the man
the bastard son of Shaitan

Nary a man brave of heart
walks alone
on a night with one star
unto the madness it is to swoon
ravaged by the loup-garou moon

Home without Walls

There is a calm enchantment watching the waterfall
as if the mountain gave birth to a fountain
In my home without walls
my thoughts are clear but I have nothing to say
as the eagle soars, the trees serenade
All I ever wanted was a home without walls
surrender to the serenity, watching the waterfalls
powerful and limitless like an endless dream
where time and imagination are free
this picture is painted in my mind
now a story in my eyes
the sun shines on the waterfall
in my home without walls
moments are fleeting like falling stars
following the beaten path has taken me too far
and love has only broken my heart
I listen closely to a familiar song
my only crime is holding on too long
so I raise a fist to those who would imprison me
in this life, no one makes the decision for me
sweet winds of freedom are calling my name
I will follow them to an early grave
freedom comes with wisdom
passed on to you in this vision
All I ever wanted was a home without walls
surrender to the serenity, watching the waterfalls
powerful and limitless like and endless dream
where time and imagination are set free

Heather

If we could go back in time and change one thing, what would
    it be?
I think for a minute and then the answer comes quite easily
I wouldn't go back to the day I left, I would go back to the
    day before
I want to see you smile again and I don't want to hurt anymore

This house is not my home
I'm leaving, though I have nowhere to go
I watch you play from behind the kitchen door
try to find a reason why I'm not a part of this anymore
when you look at me I'm afraid you knew
this would be my last memory of you

The saddest sound I'll ever hear
is the sound of silence cause you're not here
I hear your voice in my dreams and it's loud and clear
The saddest sound you'll never hear
is my heart crying and only I can hear
I have a wounded soul that's slowly dying
inside my heart is crying

Leaving is the hardest thing to do
will this be the last time I watch you come home from school
you are the reason I did all I could do

the reason it lasted many years instead of a few
I know you are going to hate me
I know you are going to blame me
All I will ever hear is, "daddy explain this to me"
you were only ten years old
I wonder how many lies you will be told

Time for me to go
we started this journey together but I must finish it alone
I wanted to tell my baby girl, "it will be alright"
we will looking at the same moon tonight
I wanted to say good-bye
but I'm sure you would not want to see your dad cry
through it all my feelings have not changed
if I live to be a hundred and one
have four more daughters and sons
you can not be replaced

If we could go back in time and change one thing, what would
    it be?

Horizontal Rain

We think we are free when we cannot see the chains
we think we are right but our children live our shame
we look on in fantastic horror at the colliding trains
everyone stops to watch the horizontal rain

Five years old, four blocks from home
he ends up missing
thirteen he dyes his hair, pierces his lips
cause his parents aren't listening
fifteen and no one understands
he sits alone with a gun in his hand
this virus is feeding on the silence
with meticulous precision, he makes a decision
he's tired of the lies hiding behind smiling eyes

Palms are sweating, there is a lump in his throat
he shoves the gun under his coat
teacher says he hasn't listened to a word she has said
he leaps to his feat, empties the chamber, shouting God is dead

Eighteen and army green
wakes to bombs bursting in the air
innocence lost while our leader counts the cost
the nights are illuminated by the rockets red glare
toe tag and body bags, no one remembers his name
another son dies too young
with little time from cradle to grave
everyone stops to watch the horizontal rain

Epilogue

Centuries ago the Gods chose a monster to guard the gates of Hell
If he could speak, these are the stories he would tell.
The beast who will remain nameless
he who slays our fiercest creations
has contained them in written word on these pages

Thank you so very much for reading *Tales from Behind Your Wall of Dreams*. This is the first installment in a series, the second installment is under construction Titles such as; "Iram Dei" Latin for Wrath of God. Our story centers around brothers returning from a four-year tour in Afghanistan, Marines. The older is wicked smart, the younger a brawler. The older uses his superior intelligence to work his way up in law enforcement; the younger is lured into the underground world of bare-knuckle fighting. Together, they decide to track down unsolved cases involving murderers, rapists, and other degenerates. The second is entitled, *House by the Cemetery*, an urban legend has it that a century-old house has millions of dollars in gold stashed away somewhere. Three unfortunate youths break in, and are now in a fight for their lives, and can't get out. The third is entitled, *My life with a Narc*, narcissist to be specific. In a society based on instant gratification and self importance, we are becoming more obsessed with our fifteen minutes of fame. In the electronic age where our kids don't get out and play, we feed them in front of the television, so we don't interrupt their game. We are not raising our kids; they are training us. In short, we are promoting narcissism. *My life with a Narc* explores the horror of these self-serving, manipulating monsters. After all, true horror is what one human being can do to another, These stories, as well as new poems such as; *Murder of Crows, Secrets and Lies, Is Anyone Listening, The Eyes of the Forest*, and *The Old Man Under the Bridge*. Thanks again for reading.

It's peaceful and serene in your sleep
        and no one will hear you scream
The best advice I could give anyone is to know who you are early in
        your life.
I just figured that out at age 63.
I am, basically, two people in one old body.
On one hand the person my hard working, blue collar, God fearing
        parents raised me to be
On the other, a product of years of mistakes and bad decisions
The school of hard knocks, if you will, or just another fool trying to
        push that rock up the hill
My own way, the road less traveled.
Except it isn't less traveled, it's crowded and littered with people
        like me
People who thought they were right too
I'm under no illusions now, I f##cked up
Misery loves company and you are only as good as the company
        you keep
My parents taught me well, both in word and deed
I just refused to listen, if only I had
So here it is in these pages, all of my mistakes
A journal of bad decisions and the pain that ensued
I'm under no illusions here either, these stories and poems are
        my mistakes
In metaphors, of course. The metaphors that define my life
The loner, the sympathetic underachiever, just trying to figure it out
Why all of my relationships, social, business or romantic
        end badly, sadly, some tragically
Regardless of the physical effort, which is the easy part
The emotional and mental part, I failed at miserably

In these stories and poems and the ones to come in the future,
are answers
Pain is a wise teacher and scars are forever
Hope you enjoyed, Tales from behind your wall of dreams

www.ingramcontent.com/pod-product-compliance
Lightning Source LLC
Chambersburg PA
CBHW061355140726
47997CB00003B/1224